For Luna and Miguel and all the young
people out there stitching together
their very own story —M. de la P.

For Steve Malk —C.L.

G. P. Putnam's Sons
An imprint of Penguin Random House LLC, New York

First published in the United States of America by G. P. Putnam's Sons,
an imprint of Penguin Random House LLC, 2022

Text copyright © 2022 by Matt de la Peña
Illustrations copyright © 2022 by Corinna Luyken

Visit us online at penguinrandomhouse.com

Library of Congress Cataloging-in-Publication Data is available.

Printed in the United States of America

ISBN 9781984813961
1 3 5 7 9 10 8 6 4 2
WOR

Design by Eileen Savage | Text set in Cooper Old Style URW
The art was created with gouache, ink, and pencil.

patchwork

MATT DE LA PEÑA
Newbery Medal–winning author

CORINNA LUYKEN
New York Times bestselling illustrator

putnam

G. P. Putnam's Sons

You were blue before you were even born.
We mark, we mark.

Your mom cut into a two-story cake
and out spilled blue,
and everyone hugged and pointed
toward the cloudless blue sky
because it was a sign.

And here you are today,
blue dressed in blue.

But sometimes your paintbrush at school
hovers above the pink.
Some days so much hurt floods your eyes,
you're scared to even blink.
But tears are not pink or blue or weak—they're human.
You are human.

And when you grow up,
the color you will come to love most
is brown.

You were put on this earth to dance.
We know, we know.

Ballet, tap, hip-hop, your body bending to the beat,
leaping from note to note,
dipping into demi-plié.
You dream in one-two-three, one-two-three.

But those rhythms inside your head
are also a kind of math,
and one day you will discover coding
and change the way the world moves.

You go everywhere with a ball in your hands.
We see, we see.

You are basketball-baseball-fútbol-any-kind-of-ball,
and you were born to compete.
Even in defeat
the game feeds you,
it leads you.

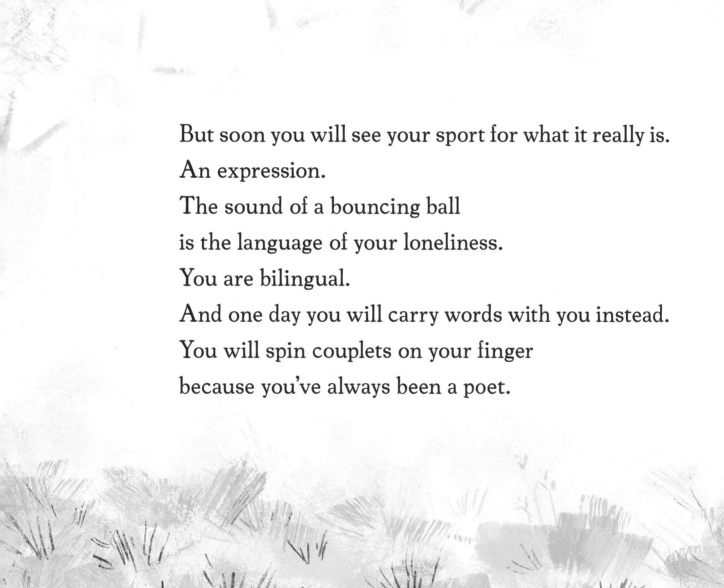

But soon you will see your sport for what it really is.
An expression.
The sound of a bouncing ball
is the language of your loneliness.
You are bilingual.
And one day you will carry words with you instead.
You will spin couplets on your finger
because you've always been a poet.

You are the kid perpetually in time-out.
We sigh, we sigh.

You shove and cut lines
and talk over teachers.
You tell jokes during the Pledge,
and your whole body buzzes
when you get a reaction.

But the skill it takes to make people laugh
is the skill you'll use to help people learn
when you become a favorite teacher.
And when a restless kid like you
lands in the back of your class,
you will see her,
you will love her.

You are kind to everyone and everything.
We beam, we beam.

When you win, it feels like a loss.
The disappointment of another is a knot
inside your stomach.
You sit beside the new kid at lunch
and give away your only cookie.

But do not mistake kindness
for a weakness.

You are a powerful magnet, pulling people.
Crowds will one day swarm to your ideas,
and they will look to you for guidance, eager to follow.
They will follow.

You are more than a single note—

played again and again.

You are a symphony.

You are sounds plucked from all the places you've been
and all the people you've met
and all the feelings you've felt.
You are blues and pinks and loneliness and laughter,
mismatched scraps accumulated over time
and stitched together
into a kind of patchwork.

And even when your pattern
loses its design,
when it grows lopsided
or tangles
or is hard to follow—

it will be beautiful.

We are beautiful.